NO

4-00

NAPOLEON PUBLIC LIBRARY

3 2930 61819 9053

WITHDRAWN

MW01042156

Bedbugs

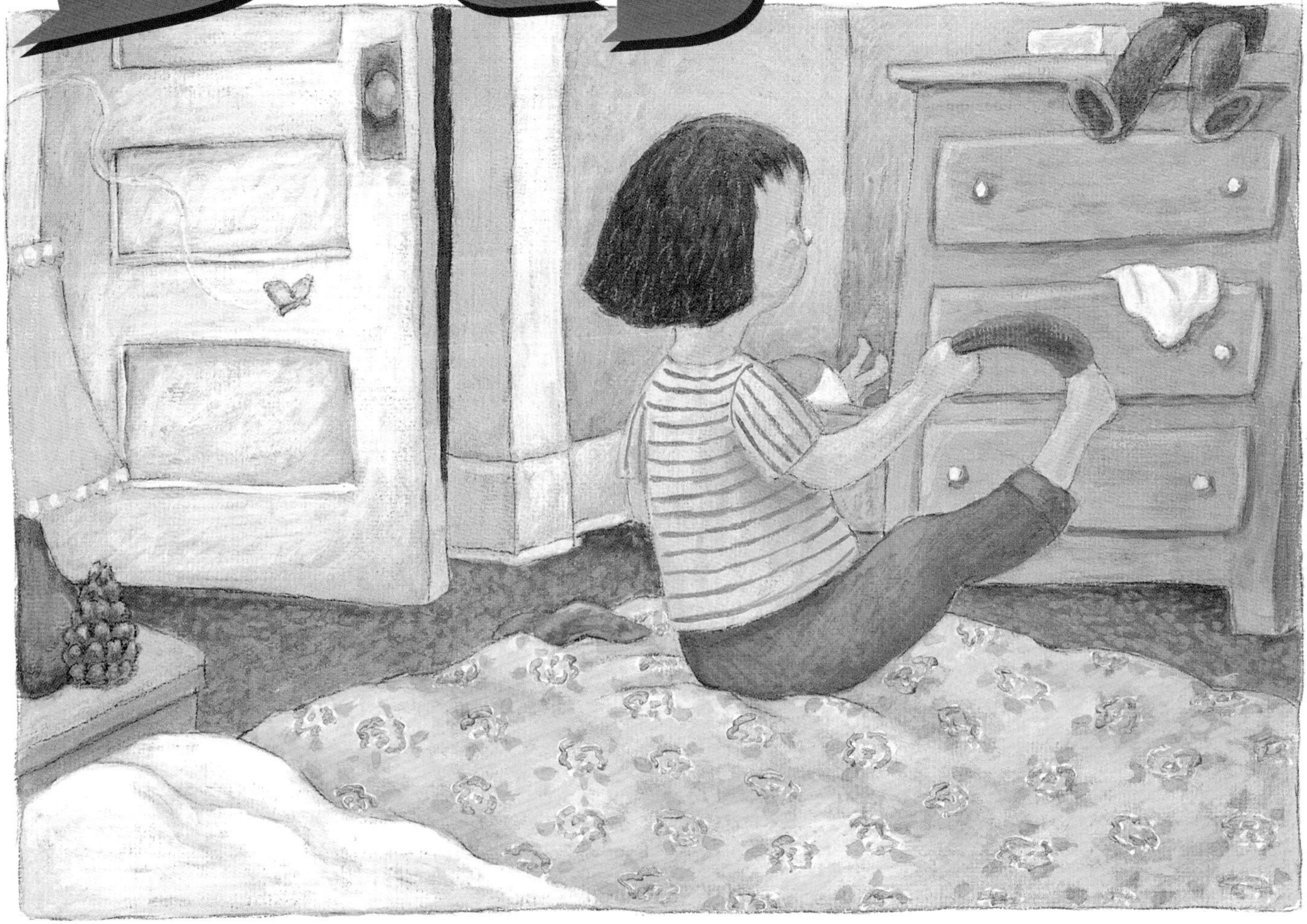

By Megan McDonald • Pictures by Paul Brett Johnson

Orchard Books • New York

For Susan–M.M.

NAPOLEON PUBLIC LIBRARY

Text copyright © 1999 by Megan McDonald
Illustrations copyright © 1999 by Paul Brett Johnson

All rights reserved. No part of this book may be
reproduced or transmitted in any form or by any means,
electronic or mechanical, including photocopying, recording,
or by any information storage or retrieval system, without
permission in writing from the Publisher.

Orchard Books, A Grolier Company
95 Madison Avenue, New York, NY 10016

Manufactured in the United States of America
Printed and bound by Phoenix Color Corp.
Book design by Zara Design
The text of this book is set in 16 point Waldbaum Book Medium.
The illustrations are acrylic reproduced in full color.
10 9 8 7 6 5 4 3 2 1

Library of Congress Cataloging-in-Publication Data
McDonald, Megan.
Bedbugs / by Megan McDonald ; pictures by Paul Brett Johnson.
p. cm.
Summary: As Susan takes her bath and gets ready for bed, she
imagines up several strange nighttime creatures that disrupt her
bedtime preparations.
ISBN 0-531-30193-1 (tr. : alk. paper).
ISBN 0-531-33193-8 (lib. bdg. : alk. paper)
[1. Baths–Fiction. 2. Bedtime–Fiction. 3. Monsters–Fiction.
4. Stories in rhyme.] I. Johnson, Paul Brett, ill. II. Title.
PZ8.3.M1463Bg 1999 [E]–dc21 99-10184

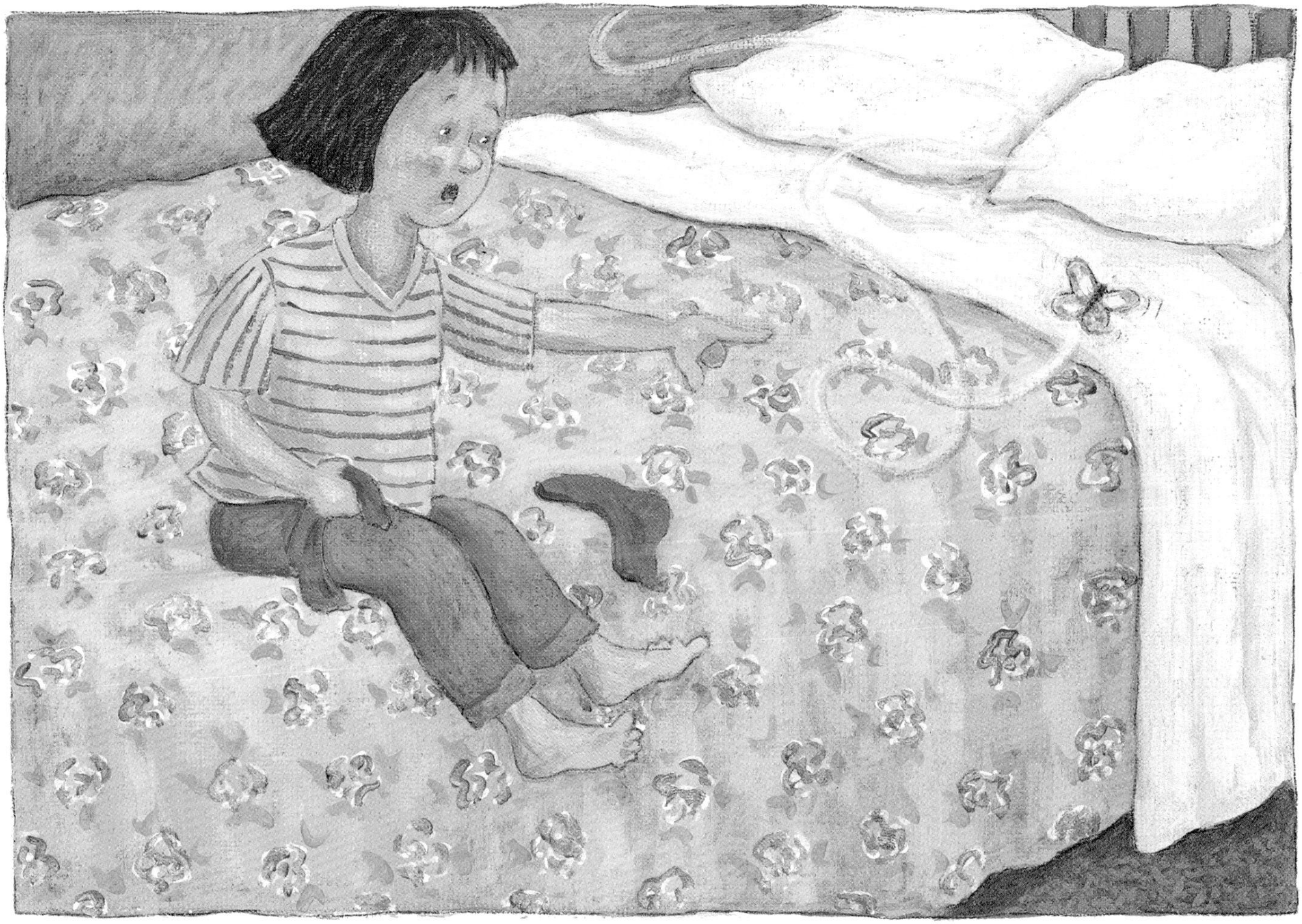

Daddy, oh Daddy,
a creature, come quick.
It's big, really big.
It's hairy and thick!

It's only a moth, honey, or a spider.

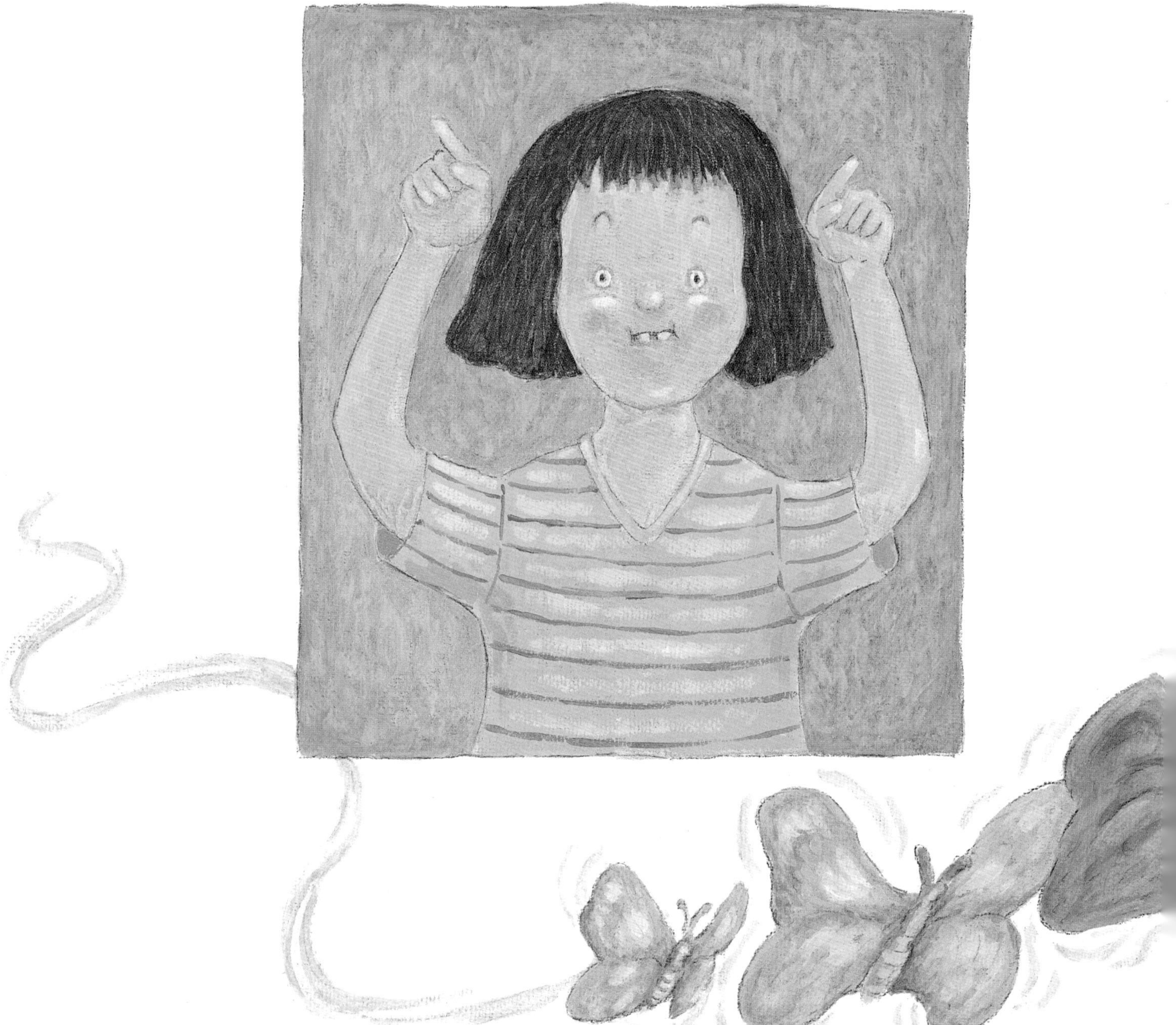

This spider has wings!
And fangs, and it's furry.
Pointy ears and bug eyes.
Daddy, please hurry!

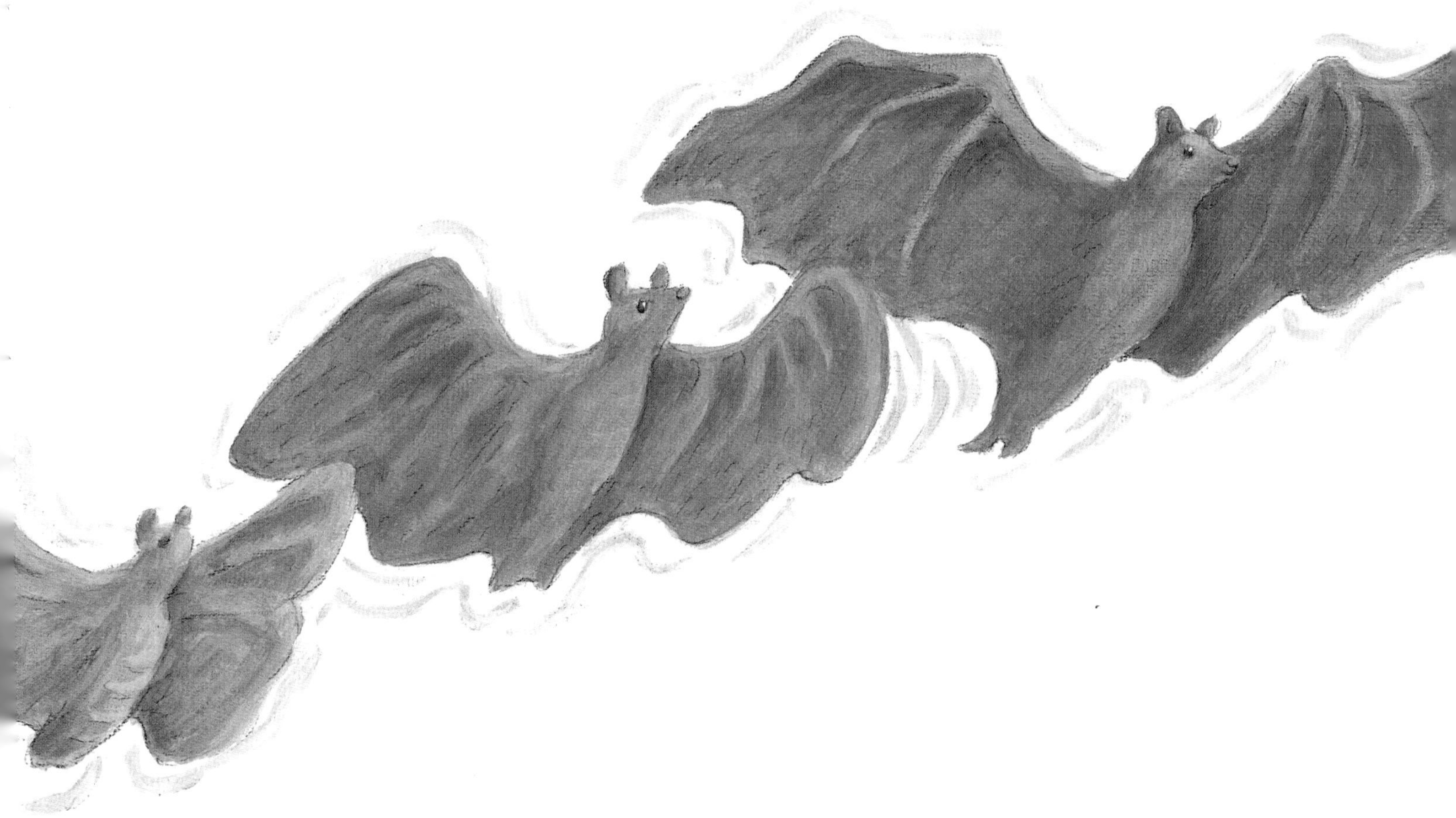

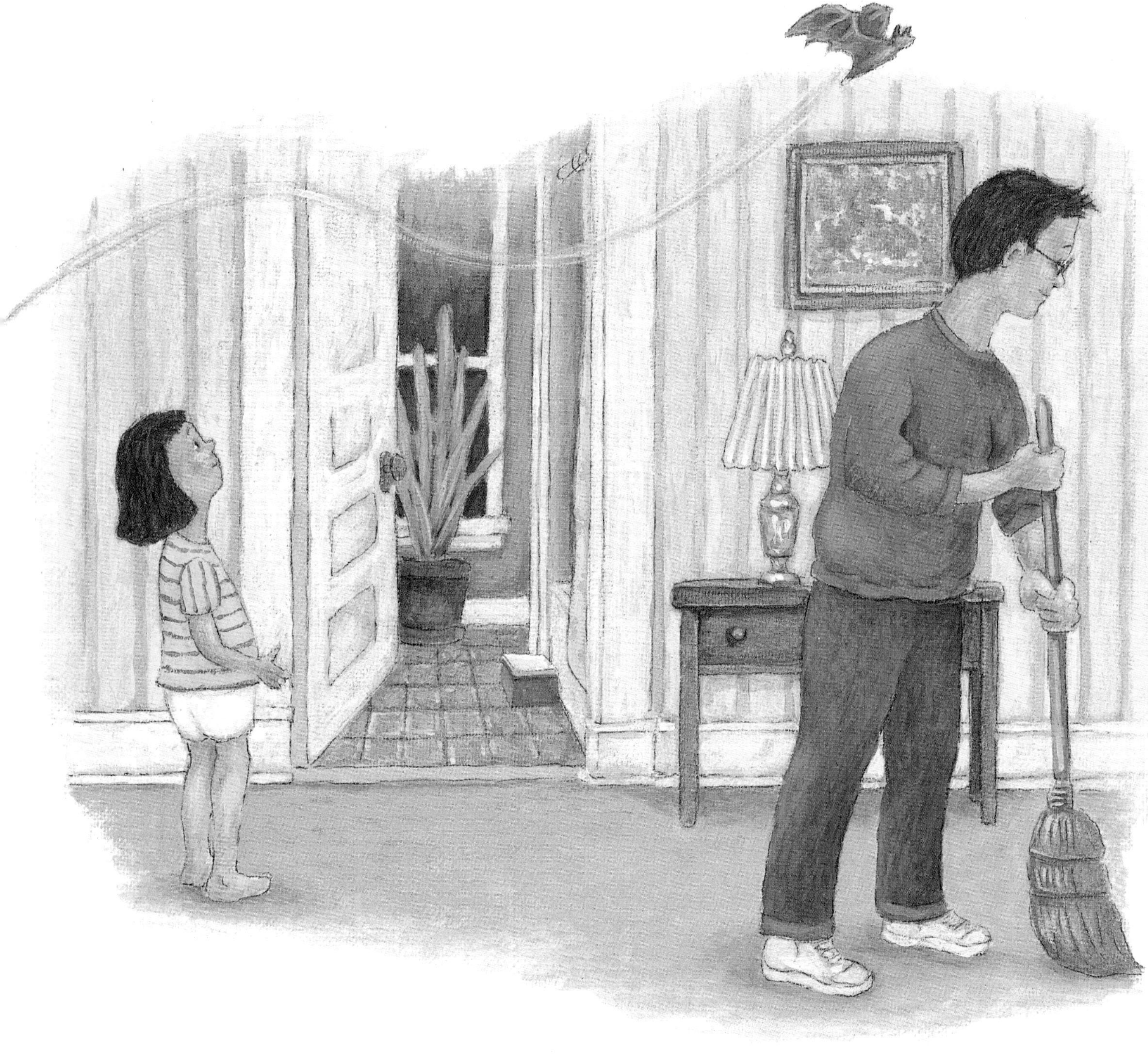

Bath time. Water's getting cold.

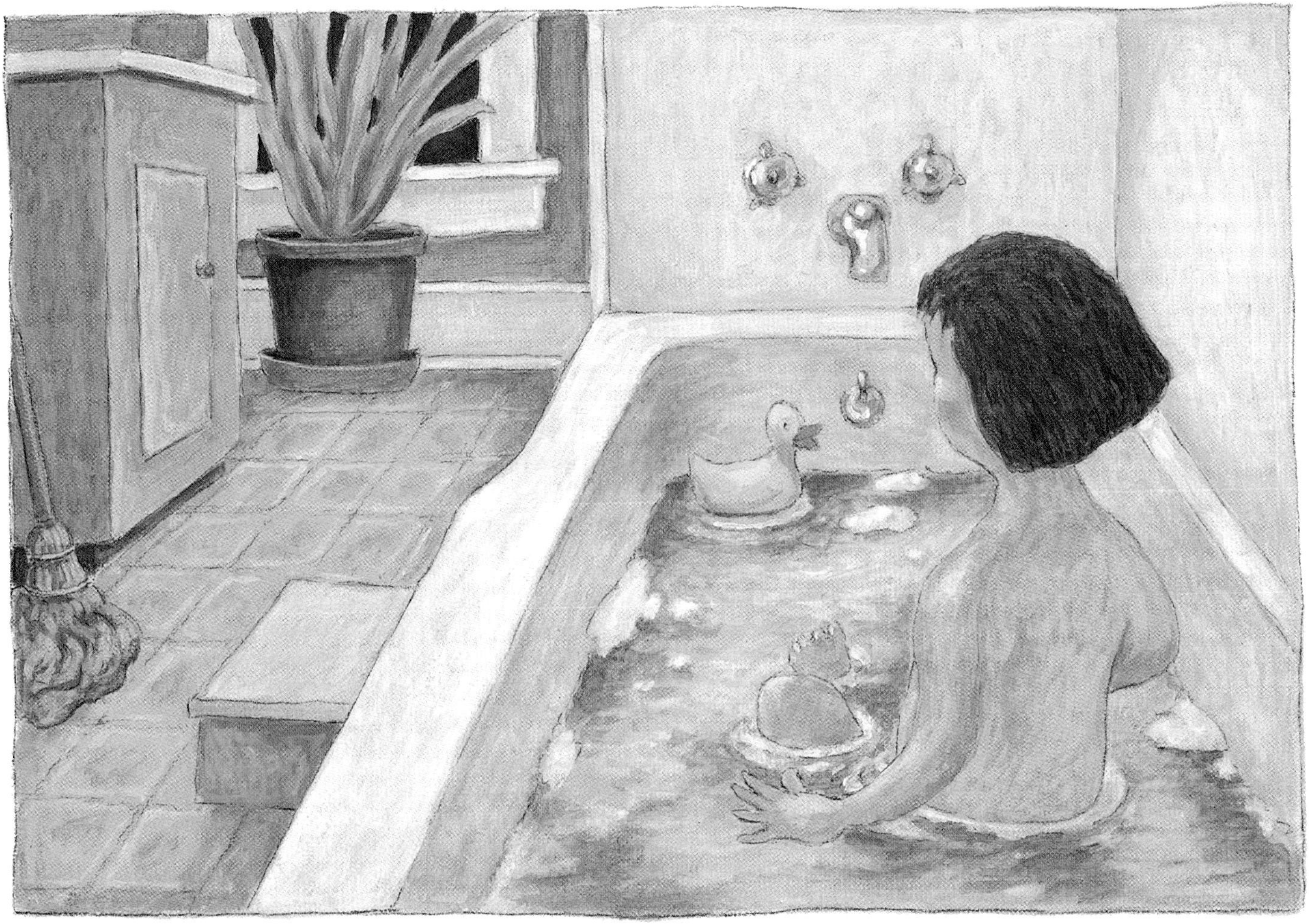

Daddy, oh Daddy,
there's a duck in the tub.
This isn't the kind
that goes rub-a-dub-dub.

Yes, Susan. . . .

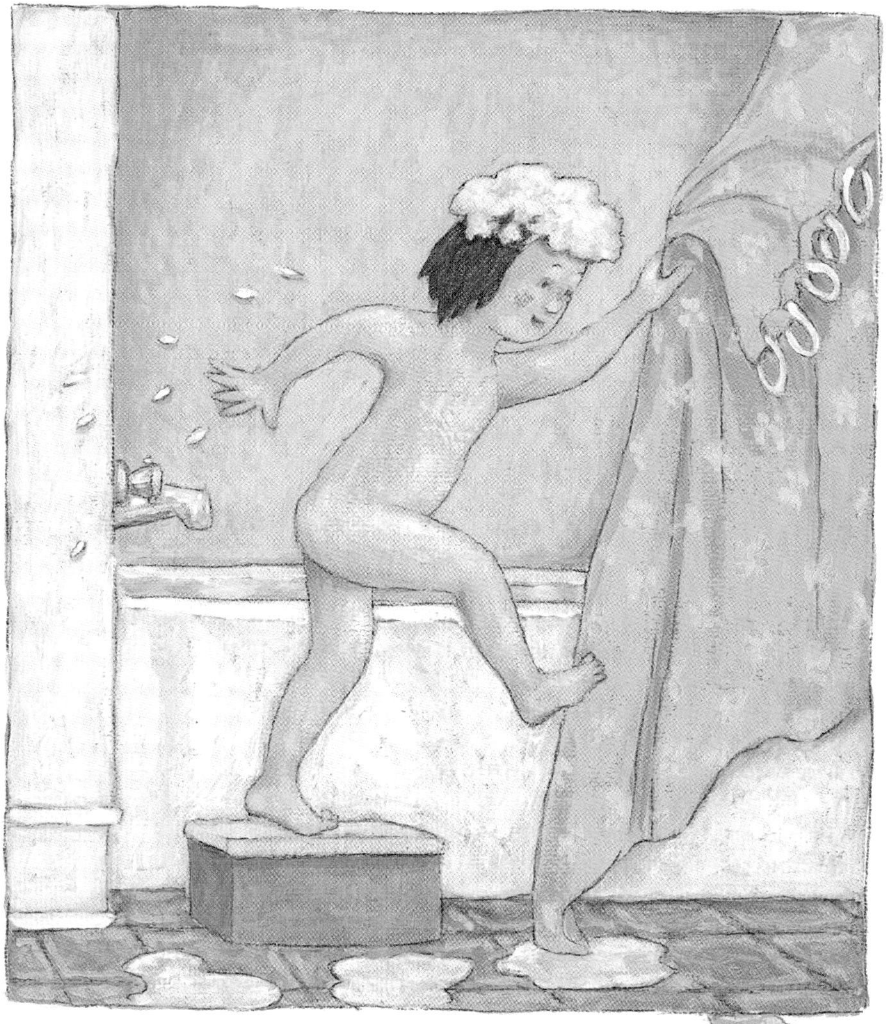

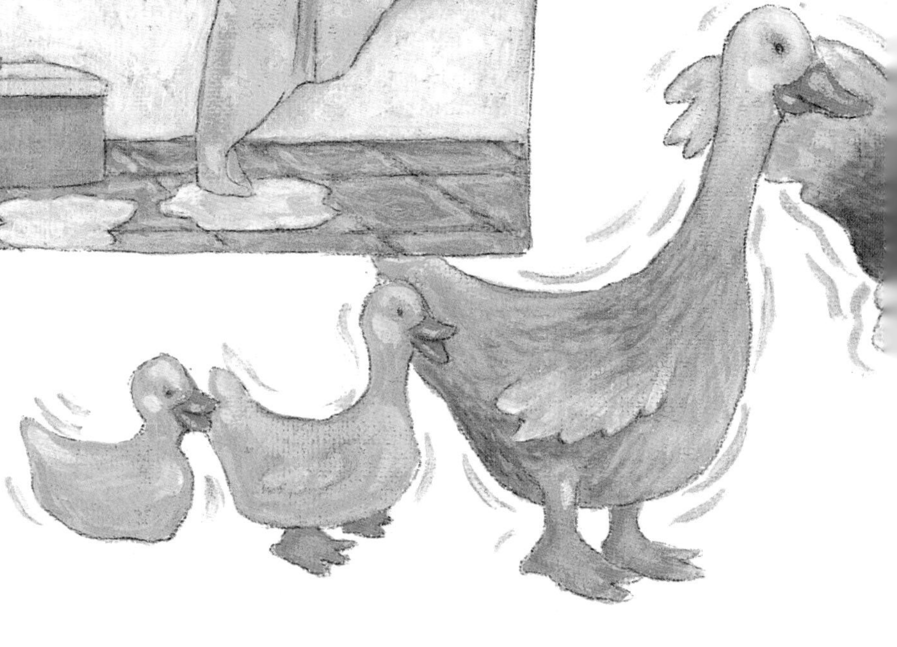

It has a bald head
the color of milk,
and it runs really fast
like Big Bird on stilts!

It's ripping apart
the new shower curtain.
Its feathers can't fly,
but it wants out for certain!

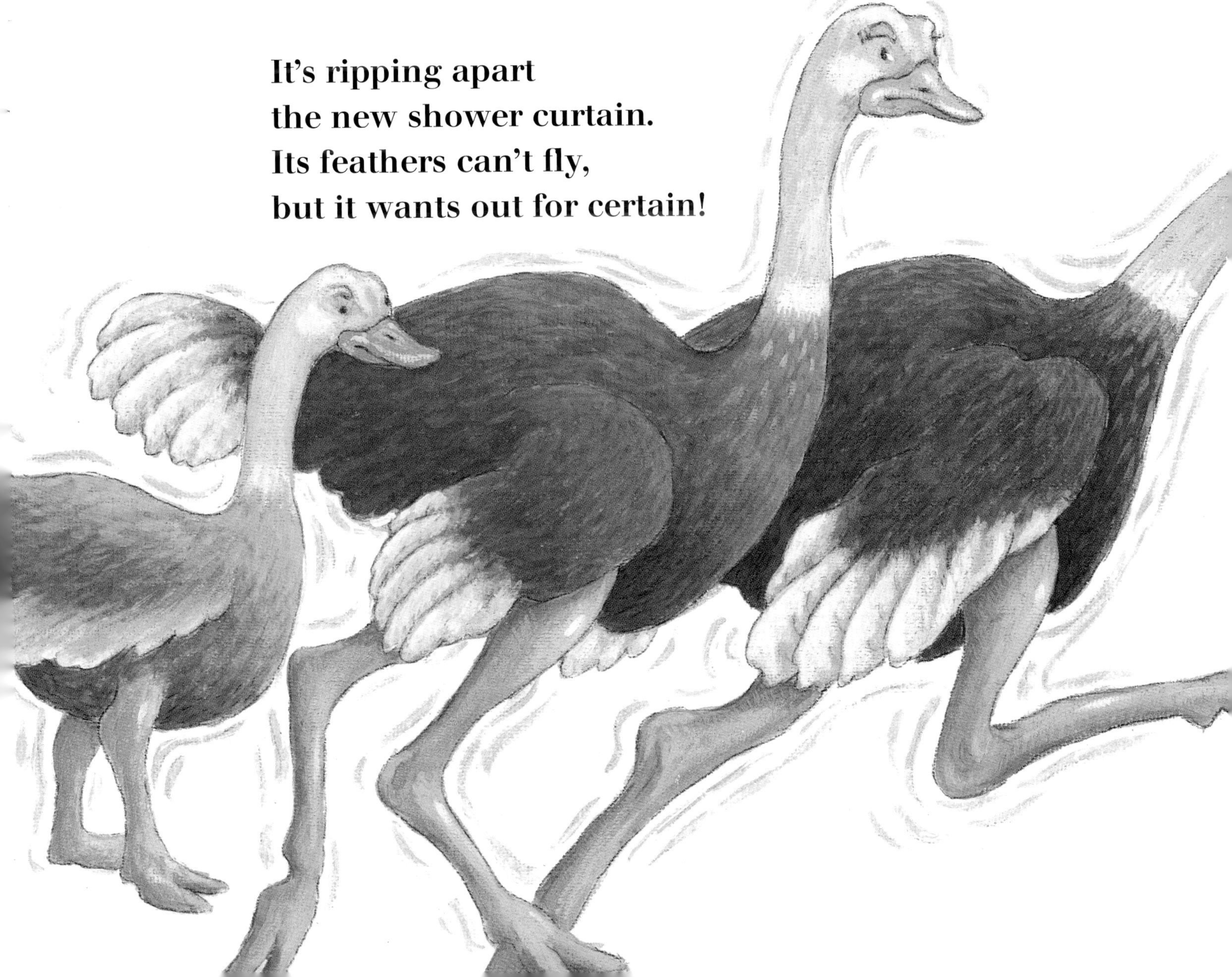

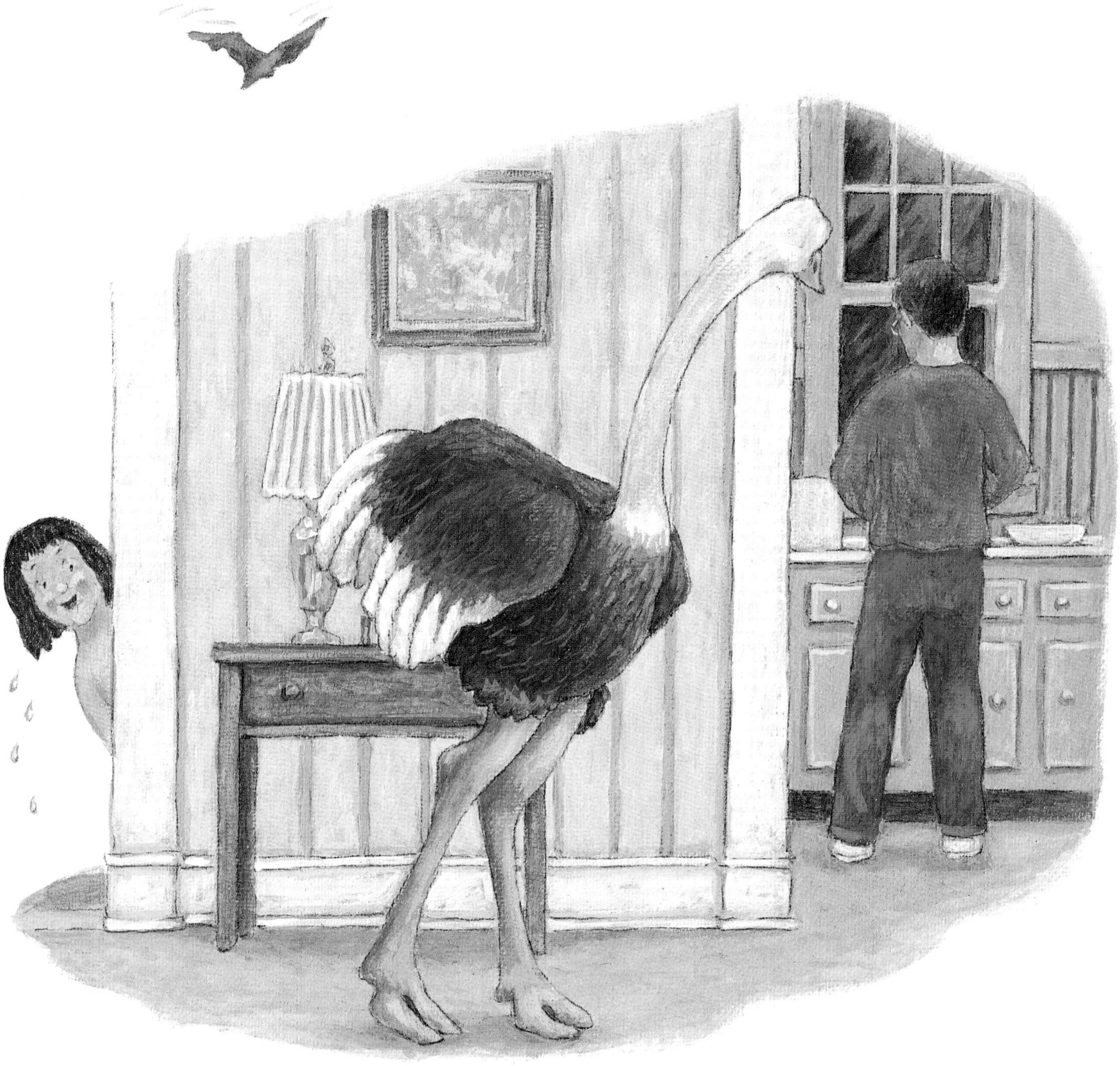

Remember, don't leave a puddle on the floor.

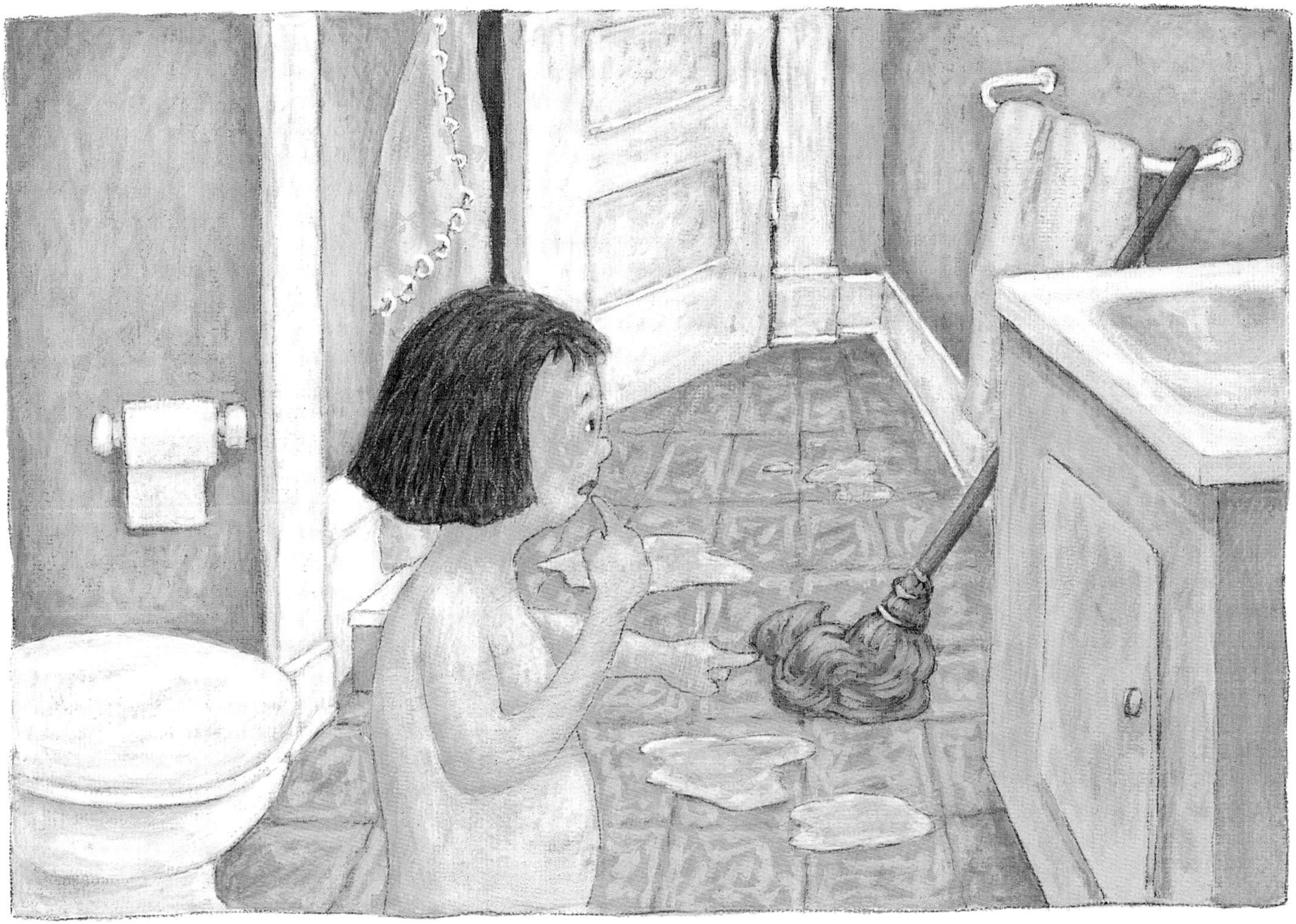

The mop! It keeps moving!
It's truer than true.
And it's squirting out blood
that's bluer than blue.

Just mop up the water, please.

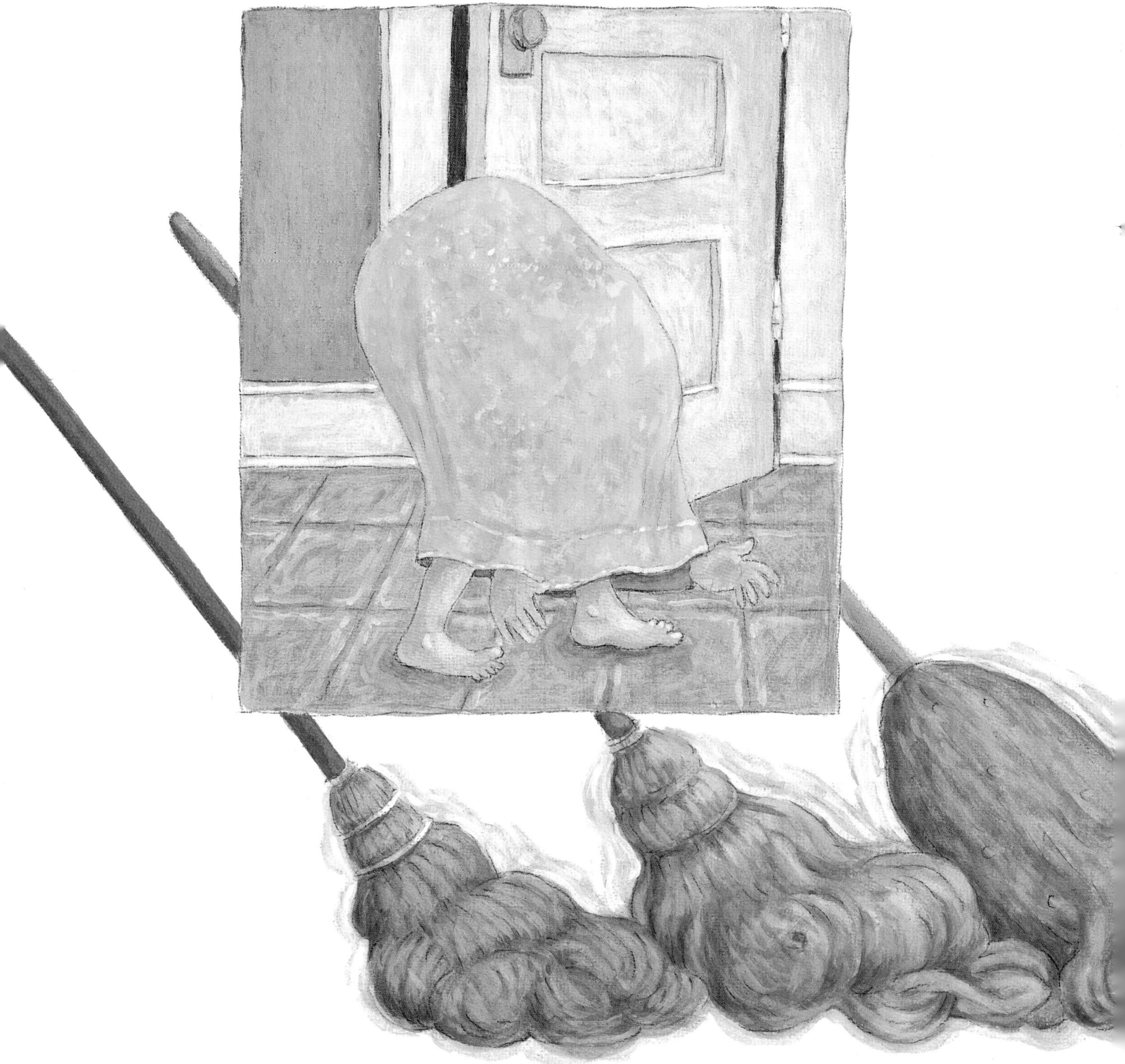

Hundreds of suckers,
speckles, and more–
spots and stripes
and arms galore!

Two plus two plus two plus two.
I counted them up to eight.
Sticky-out eyes staring right at me . . .
I don't feel so great.

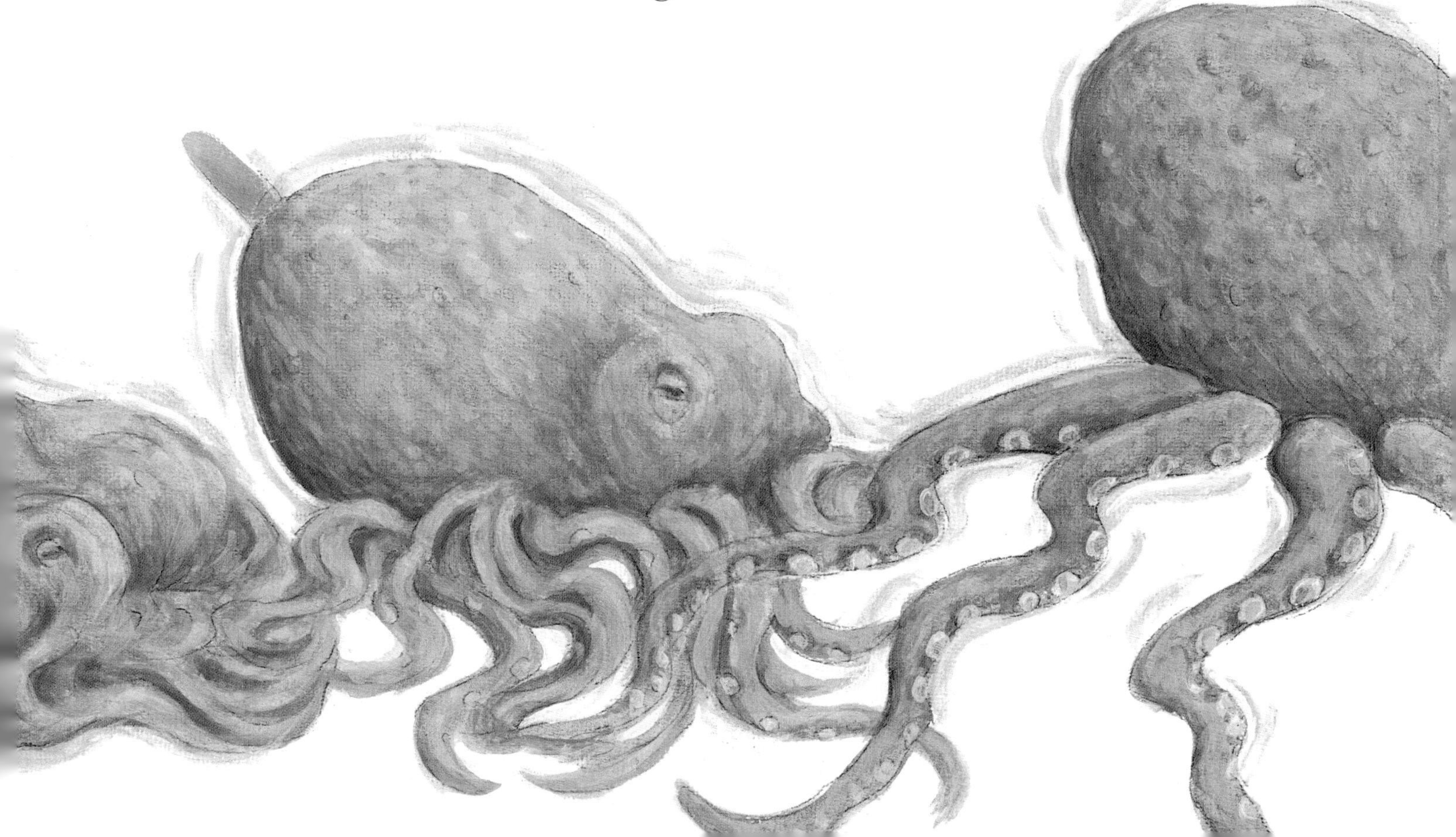

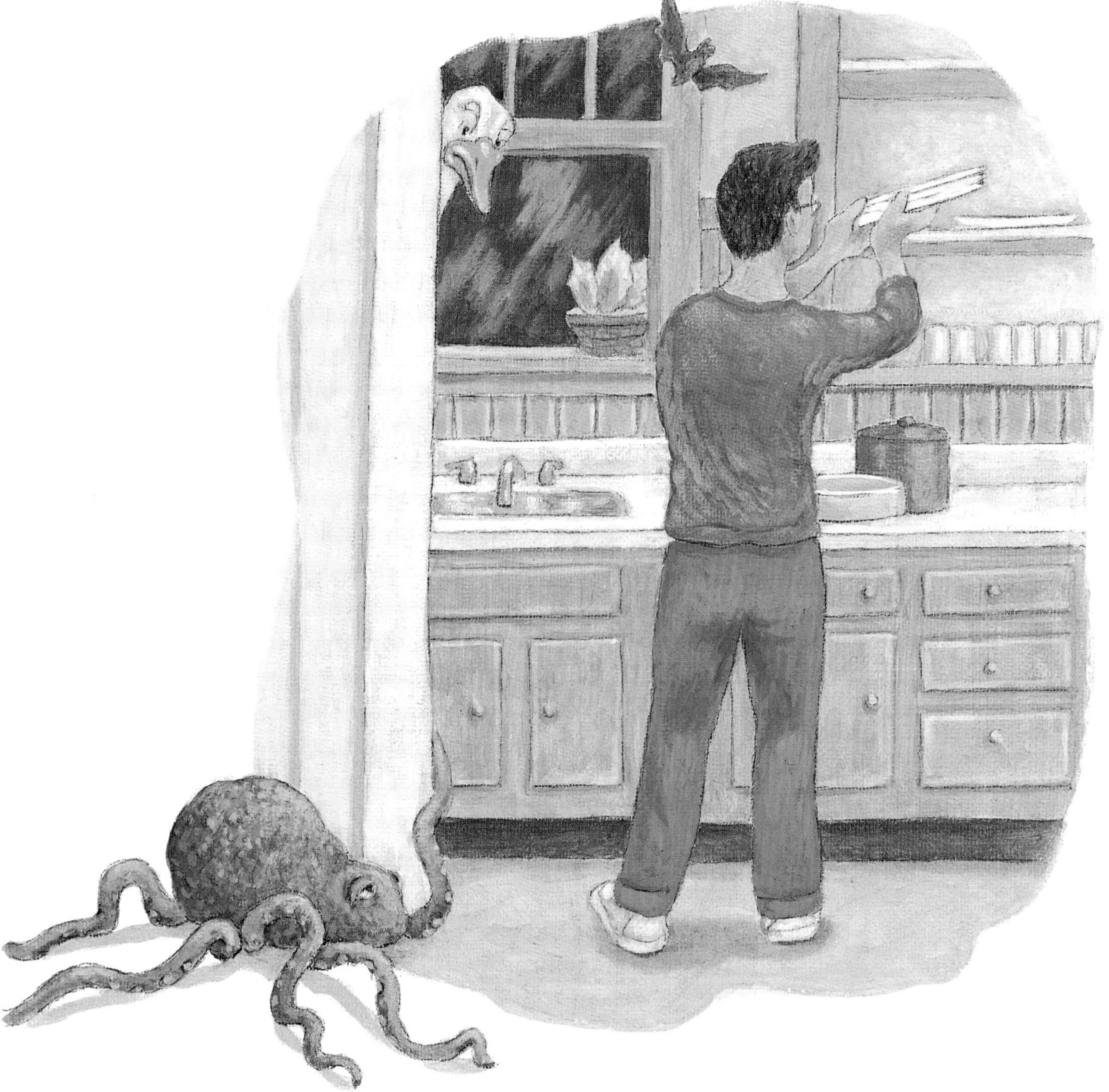

Hurry up, Susan. Time for bed.

Daddy, oh Daddy . . .

What is it now?

I can't brush my teeth—
a big shiny fin,
two more underneath!

*It's just a silverfish, honey.
From the drain.*

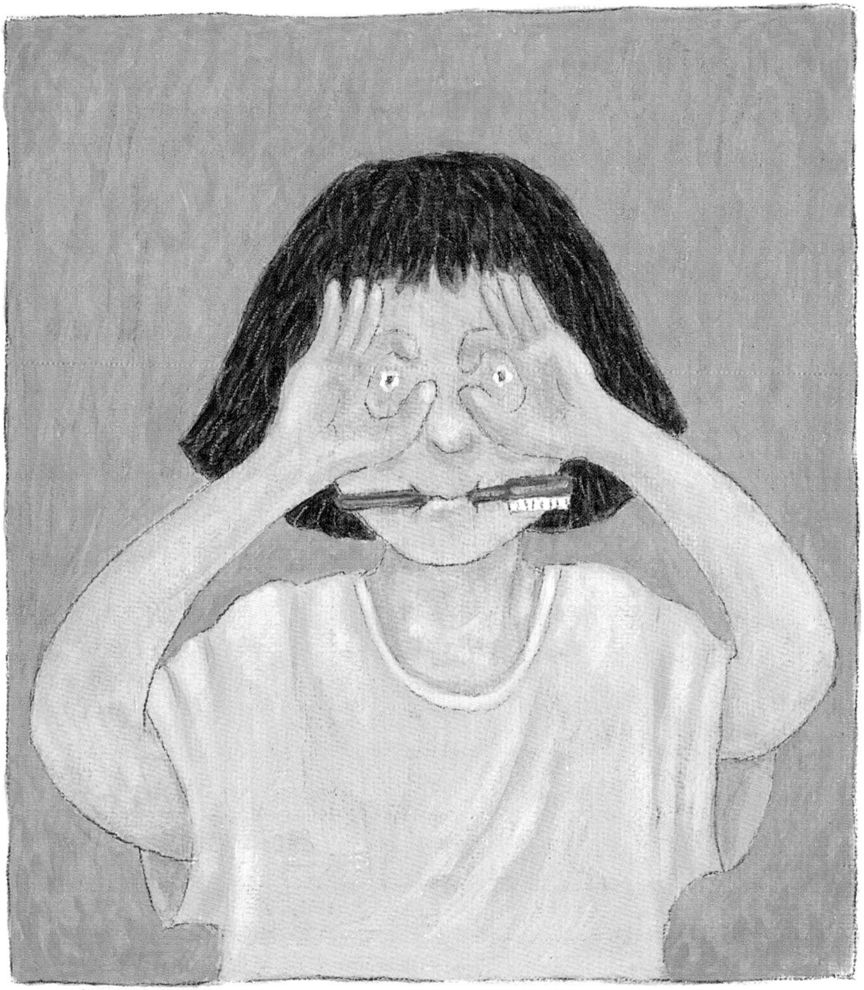

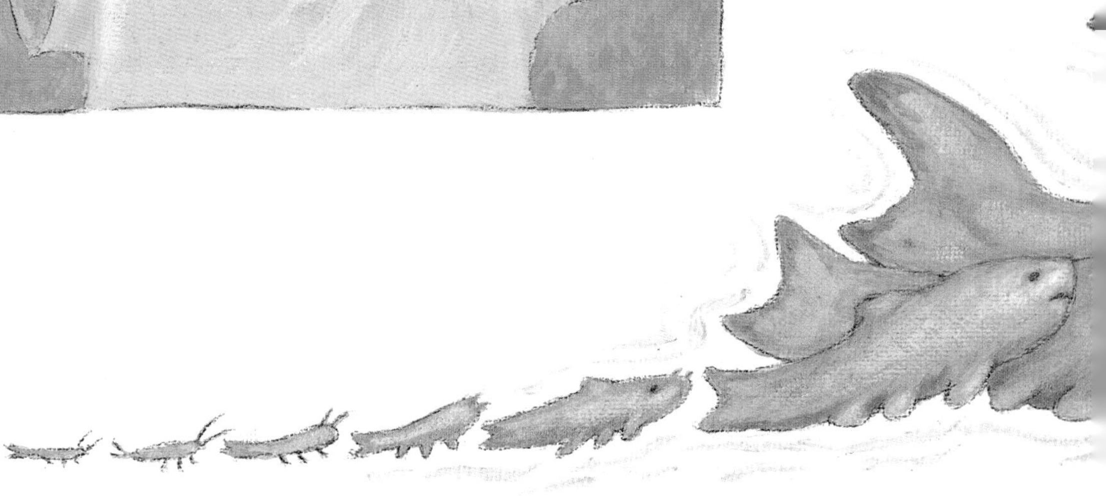

With cat eyes that shine
like the headlights of cars?
And a mouthful of teeth
that glow in the dark?

This thing's no fish
if that's what you think–
it's mean and it's fast
and won't fit down the sink!

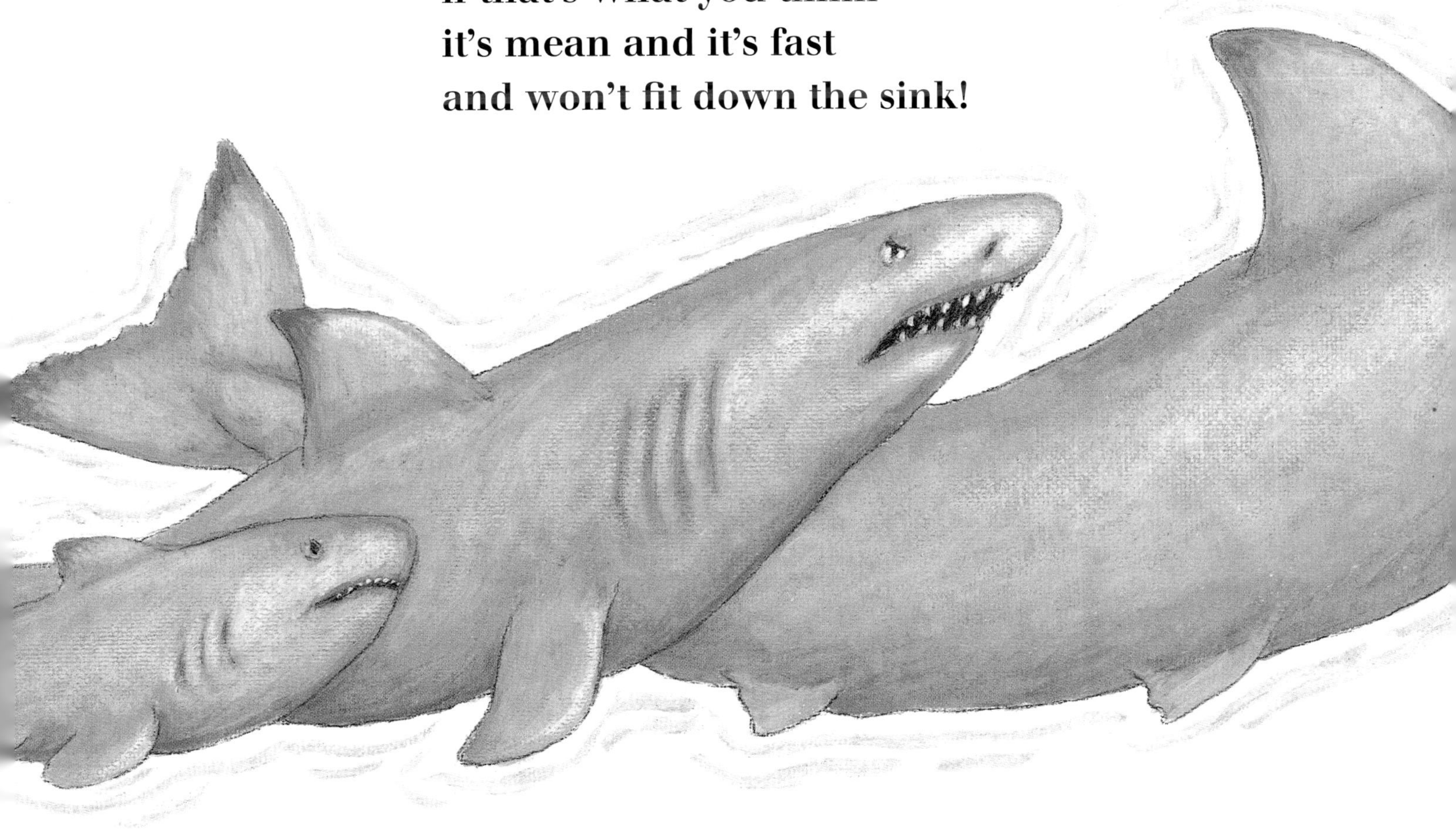

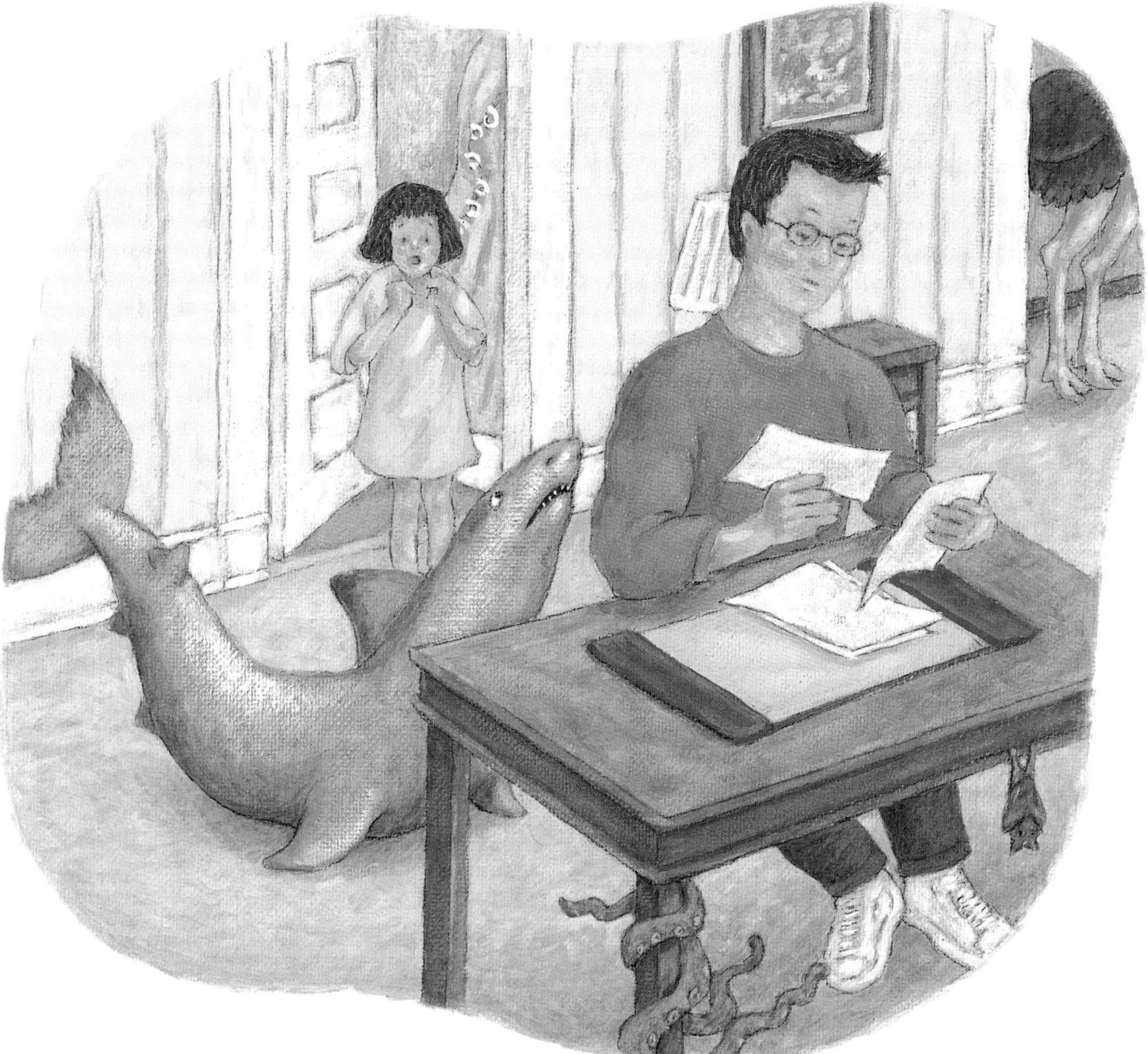

Uh-huh. Finish brushing now. It's past your bedtime.

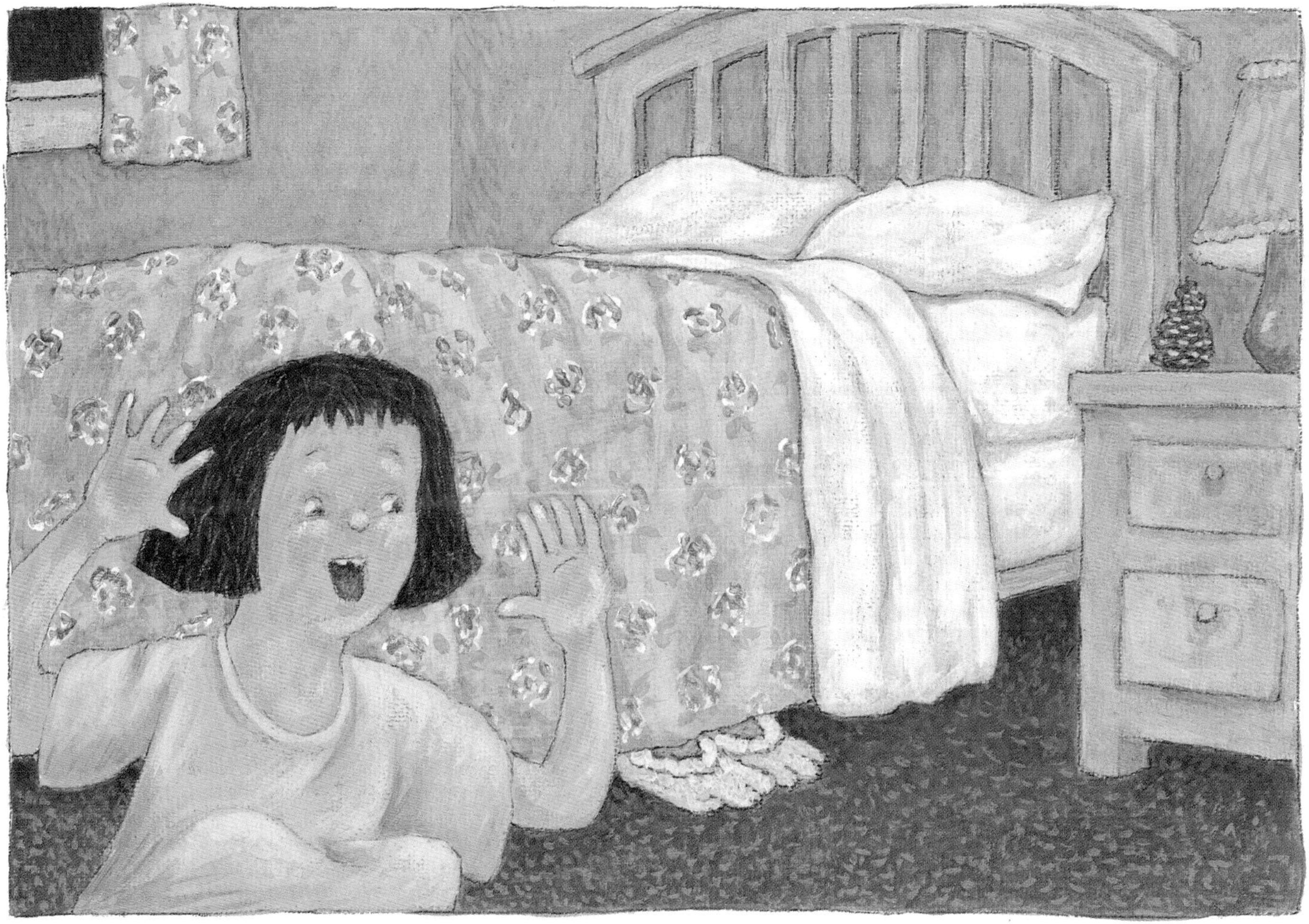

Daddy, oh Daddy,
under my bed . . .
paws and claws
and a great big head!

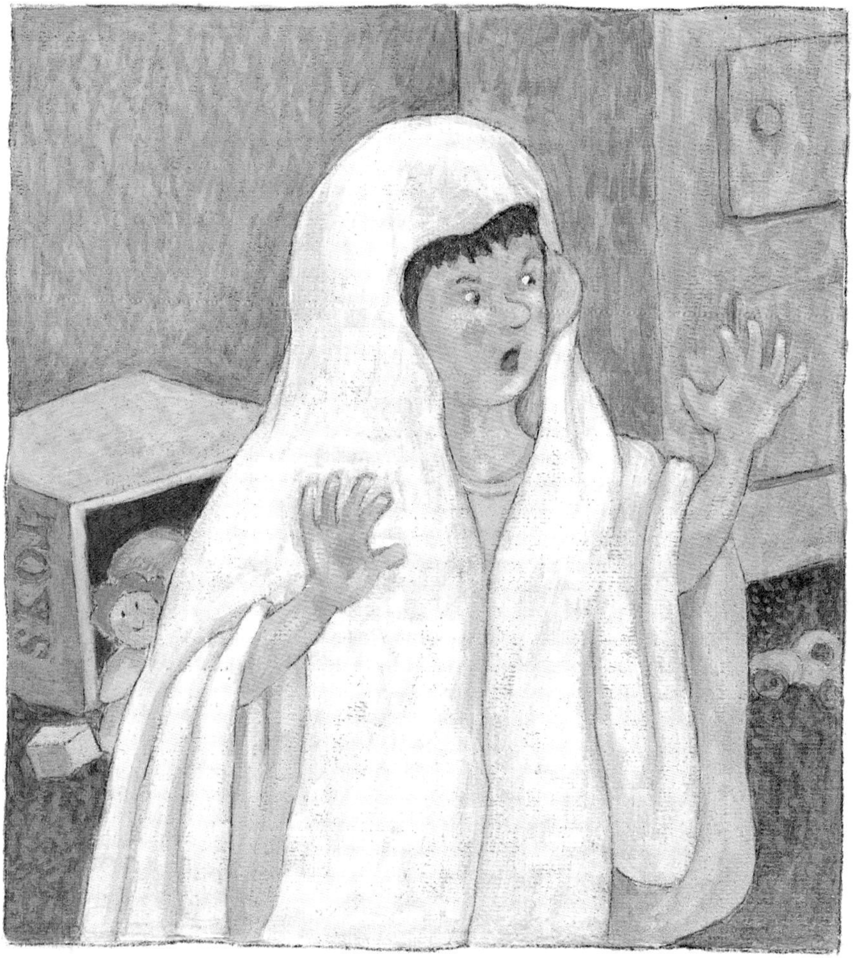
TOYS

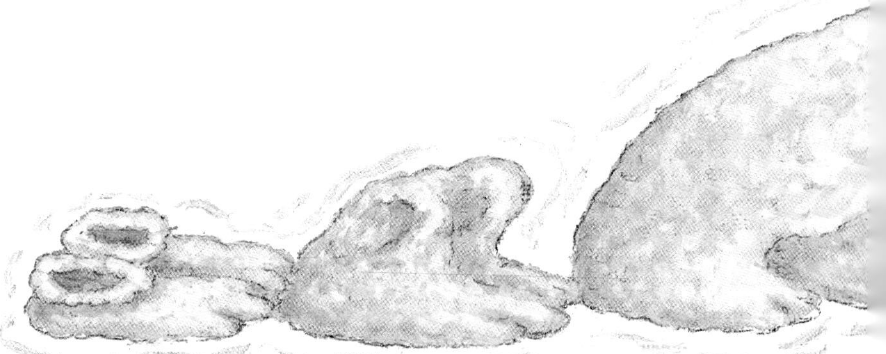

It's big and it's white,
all covered with snow.
Knocked over my toy box
in one single blow.

With the shake of its coat,
all fuzzy and furry,
I'm predicting a blizzard—
there's already a flurry.

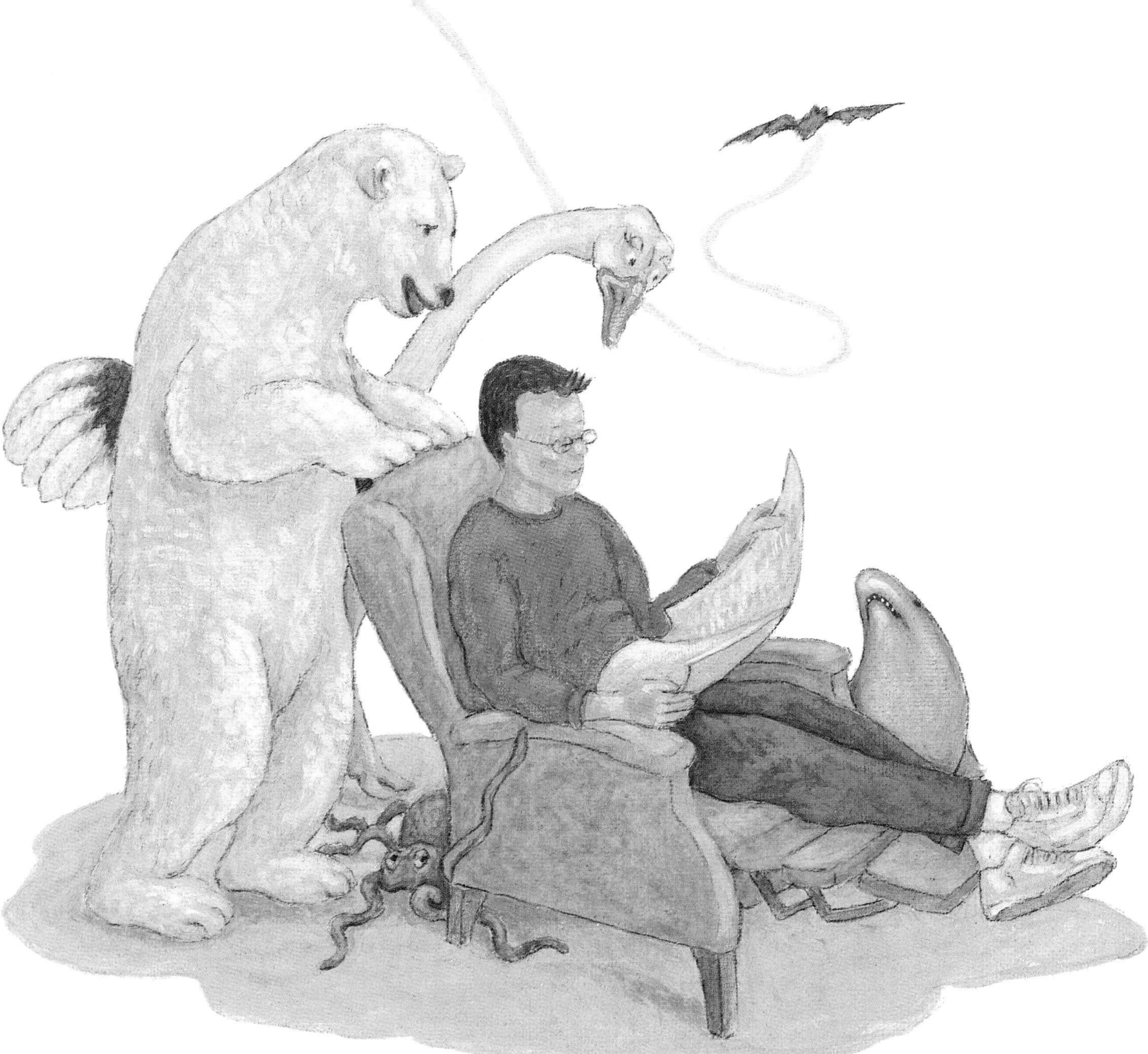

Climb in bed, Susan.
Daddy'll be right there to give you a bear hug.

Daddy, oh Daddy,
I tried counting sheep.
Honest I did,
but you'll never believe . . .

Don't tell me.
A girl-eating monster,
a fire-spitting dragon,
a five-headed cobra . . .
anything not to go to bed.

A prickly pine, Daddy!
It's alive, I'm not kidding.
A pincushion with eyes.
I see right where it's sitting.

Its back and its head
all covered with pins.
Ten thousand at least,
but this time, no fins!

Hiding under my pillow,
eating cookies and chips,
baring terrible teeth,
licking horrible lips. . . .

Okay, Susan. If Daddy comes to your room
and removes the porcupine from your bed,
will you promise to close your eyes
and go to sleep? Once and for all?

I'll go to sleep
I solemnly swear.
If you'll please move that *thing*
with orange teeth and black hair.

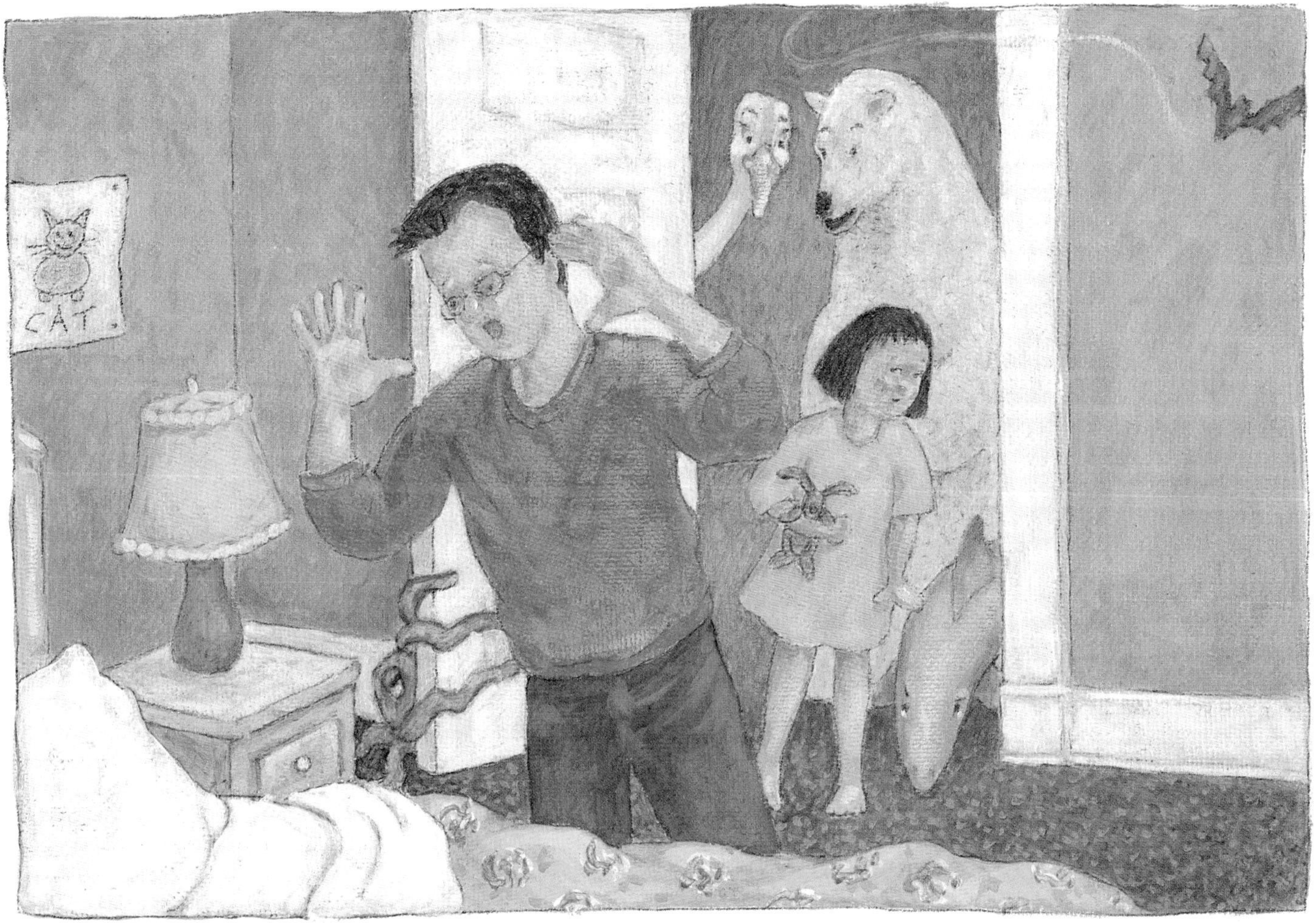
CAT

Susan, oh Susan,
hurry, come quick!
You were telling the truth.
This wasn't a trick!

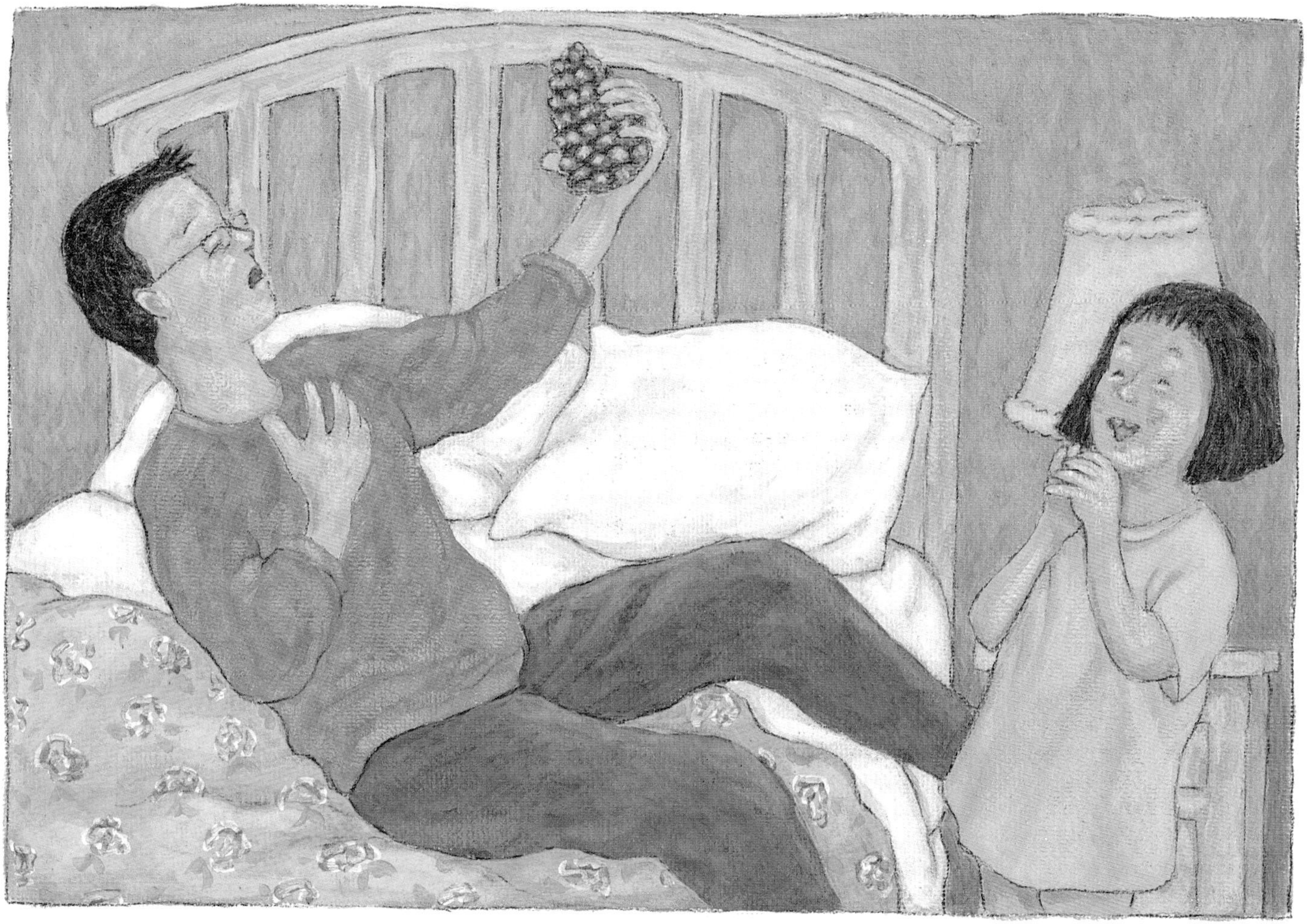

I'm covered with needles
and porcupine hair.
I feel like a cactus–
a prickly pear!

Don't worry, Daddy,
I know just what to do.
With me for a doctor
you'll be good as new.

I'll read *you* a story,
then kiss *you* good-night.

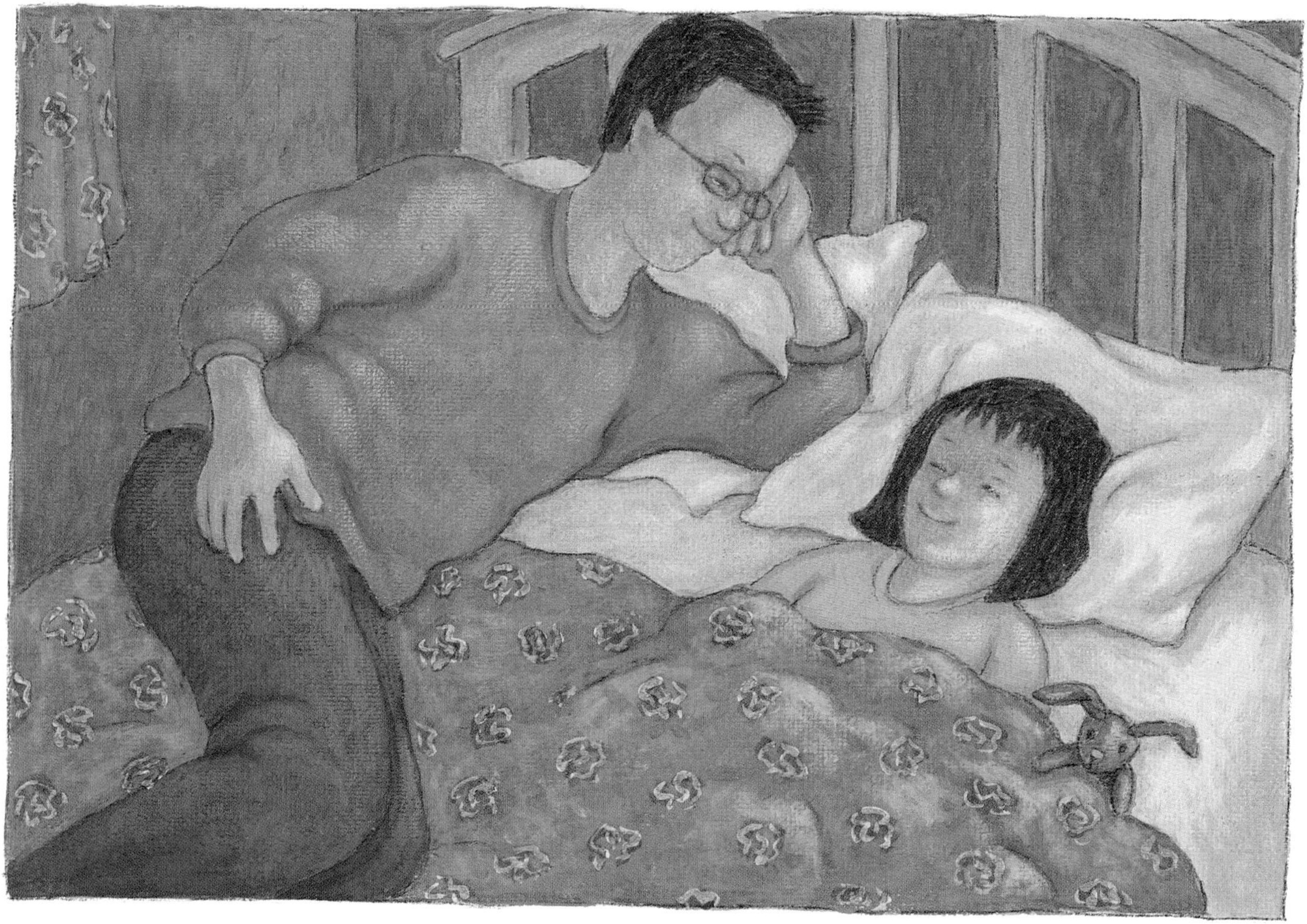

I'll tuck *myself* in
and turn out the light.

Close your eyes, Daddy.
Try to sleep tight.
Remember now, don't let
the bedbugs bite.

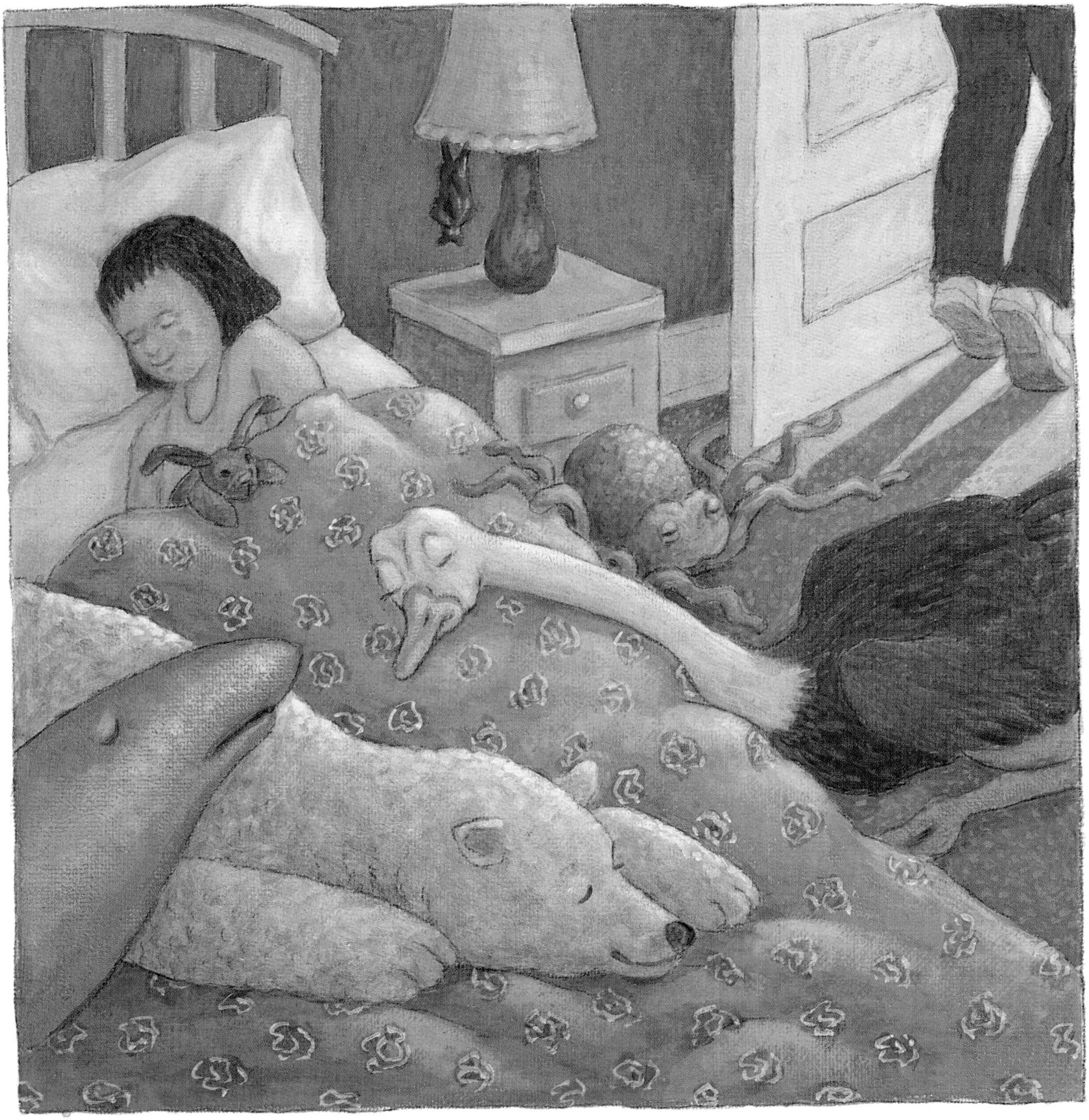

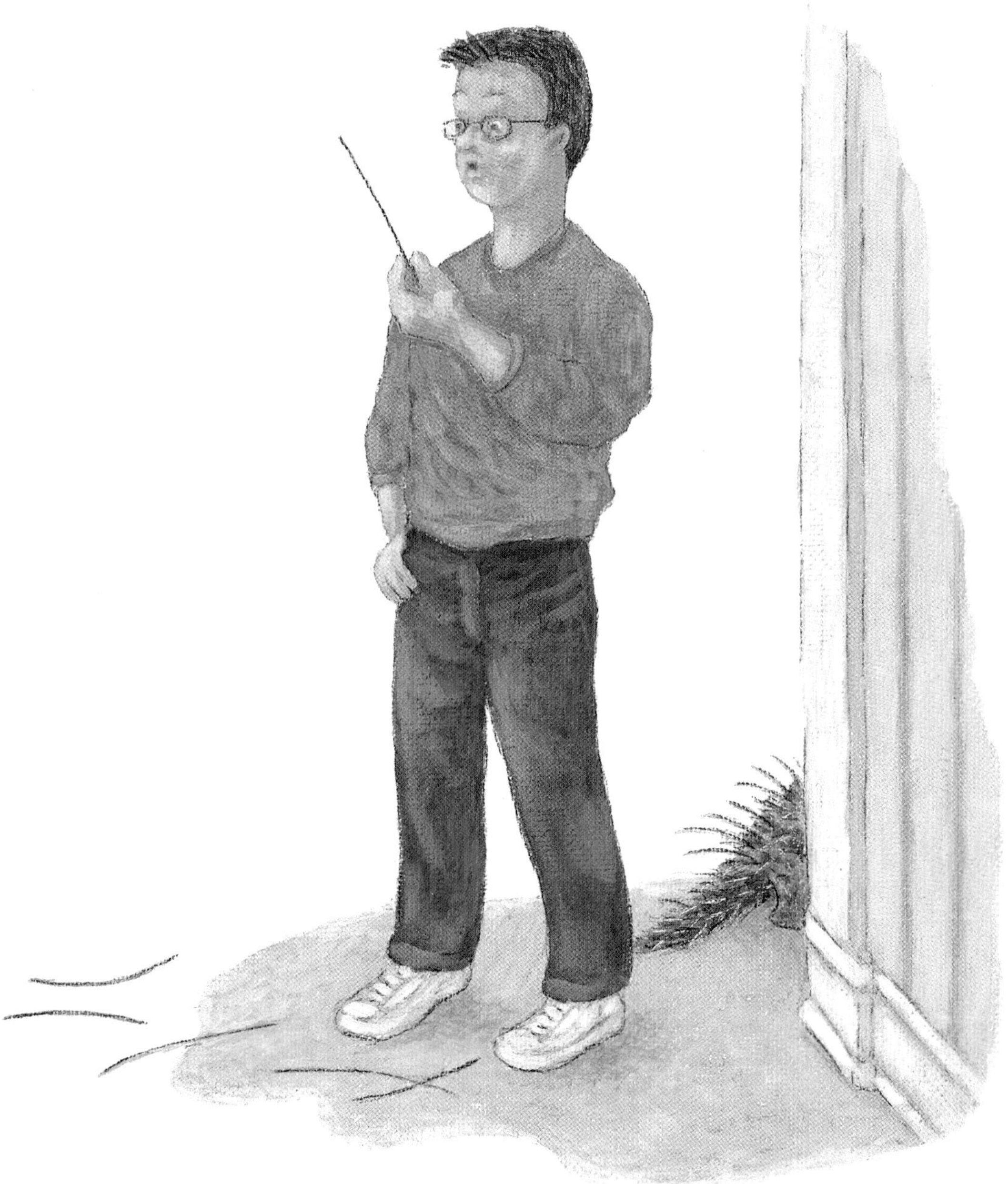